The New Scooter

Written by Dot Meharry
Illustrated by Ian Forss

Emma got a new scooter for her birthday. She took it outside to the driveway. She pushed with her foot. She pushed again and again. Soon, she could balance on the scooter. She rode it around and around.

Grandma watched Emma.
She saw Emma push with her foot.
She saw her push again
and again. She saw her ride
her scooter around and around.

Later that day, Grandma picked up Emma's scooter. She went out to the driveway.

Grandma pushed with her foot.
She pushed again and again.
Soon, she could ride
around and around
on the driveway.

The next day,
Grandma went shopping.
She came back with a big box.
Emma helped Grandma open it.

"It's a scooter just like mine!"
said Emma.

They went out to the driveway. Emma rode her scooter around and around. Grandma rode her scooter around and around.

Emma did tricks on her scooter.
Grandma did tricks on her scooter.

"Where did you learn to ride a scooter?" asked Emma.

Grandma smiled.
"I just picked it up!" she said.